Emi Isn't Scared of Monsters

by
Alina
Tysoe

Orchard Books
An Imprint of Scholastic Inc.
New York

I wonder which monster we will catch...
maybe a really BIG one?
I've been caught!
ha!

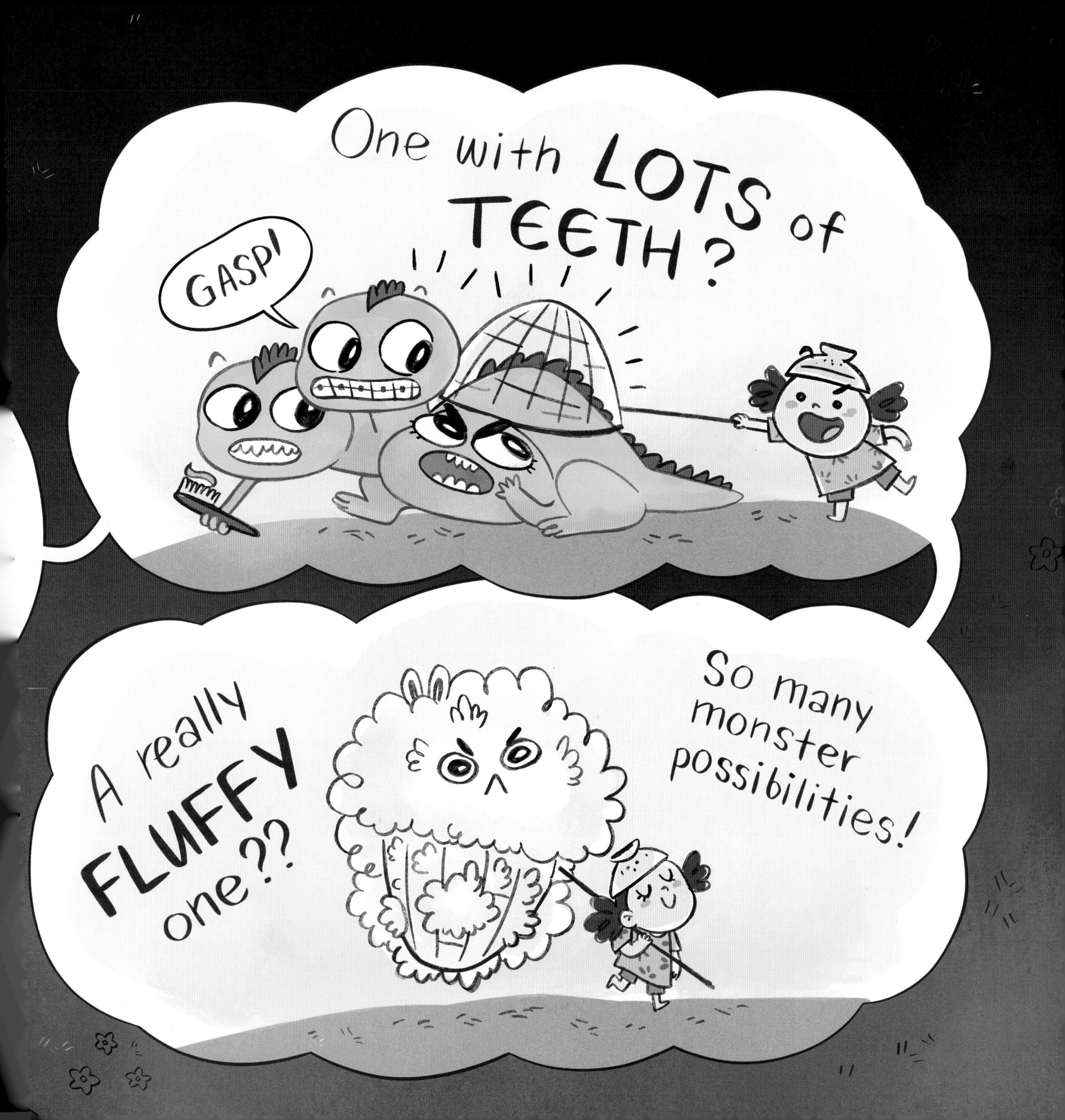
One with LOTS of TEETH?
GASP!
A really FLUFFY one??
So many monster possibilities!

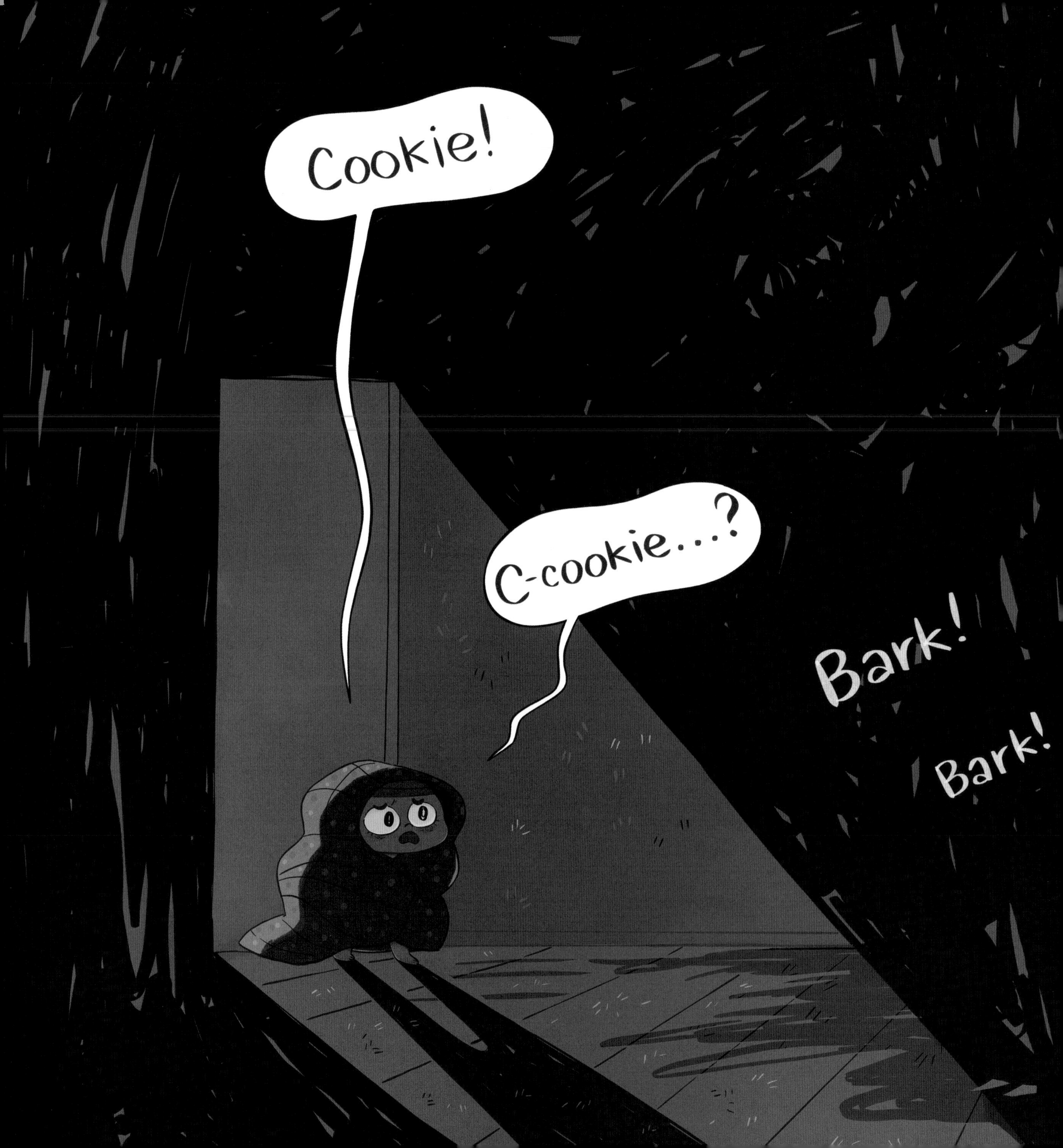
Cookie!
C-cookie...?
Bark!
Bark!

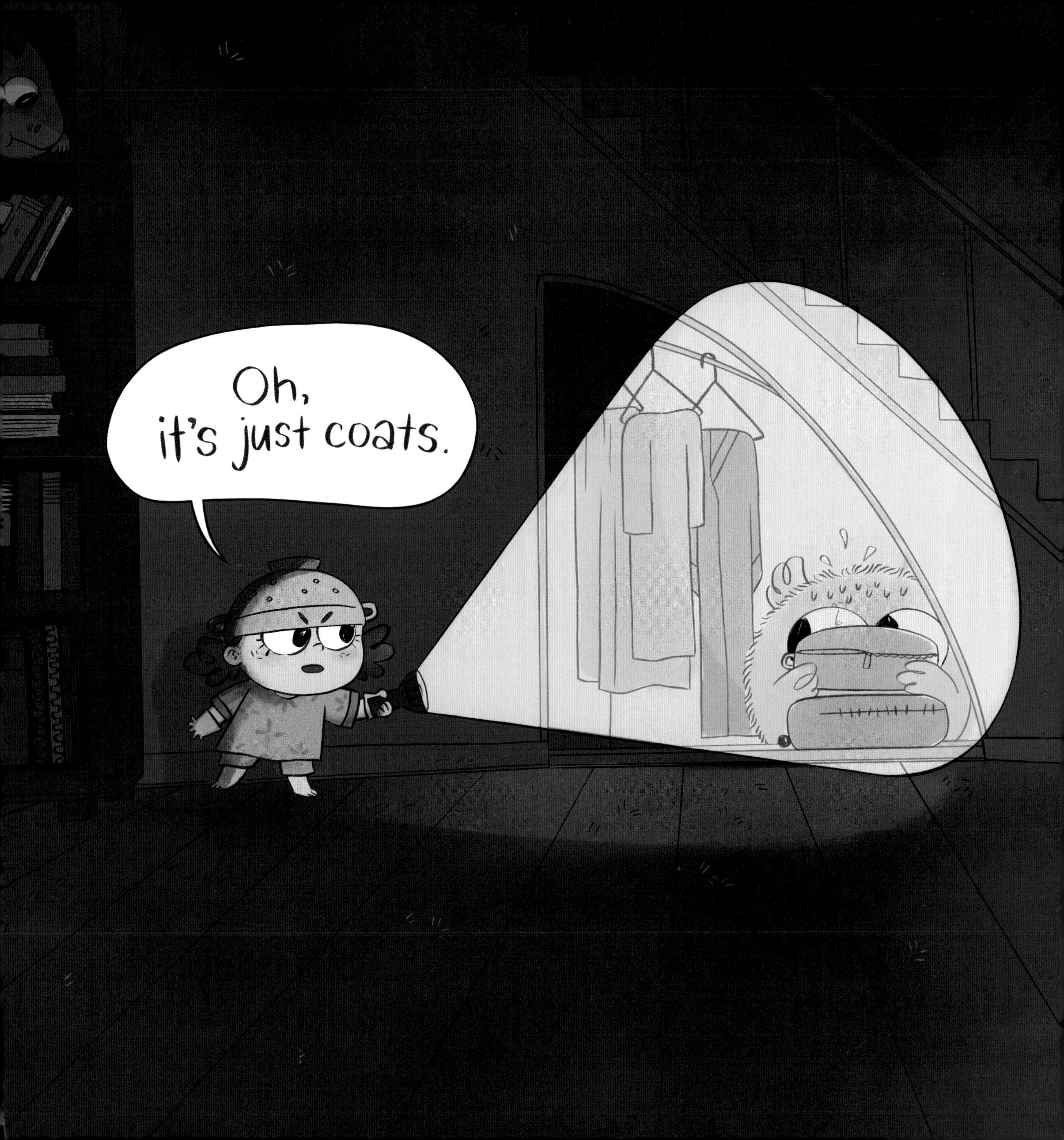
Oh,
it's just coats.

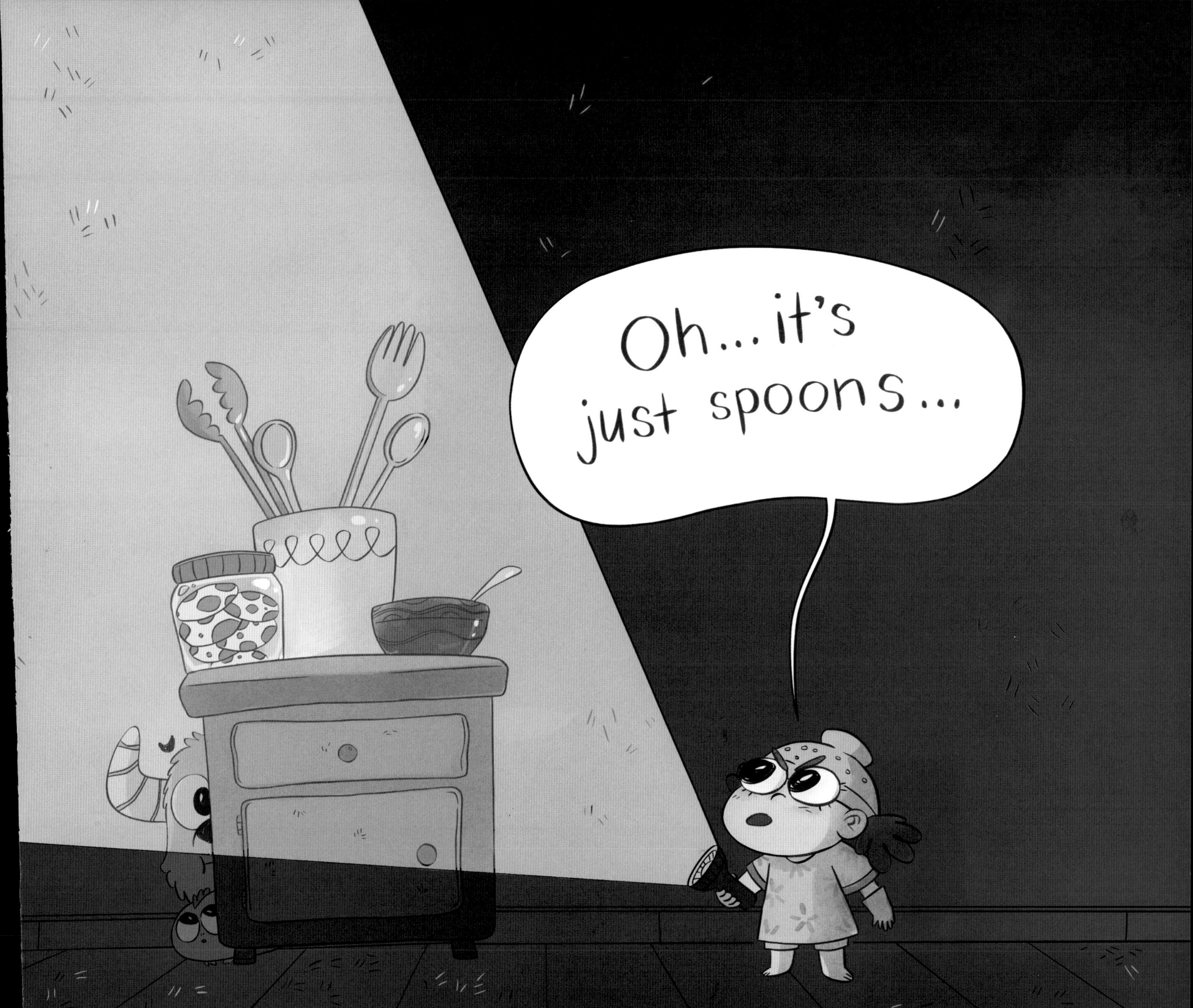
Oh... it's just spoons...

I told you, you didn't have to be scared!
There aren't even ANY monsters here. So boring.

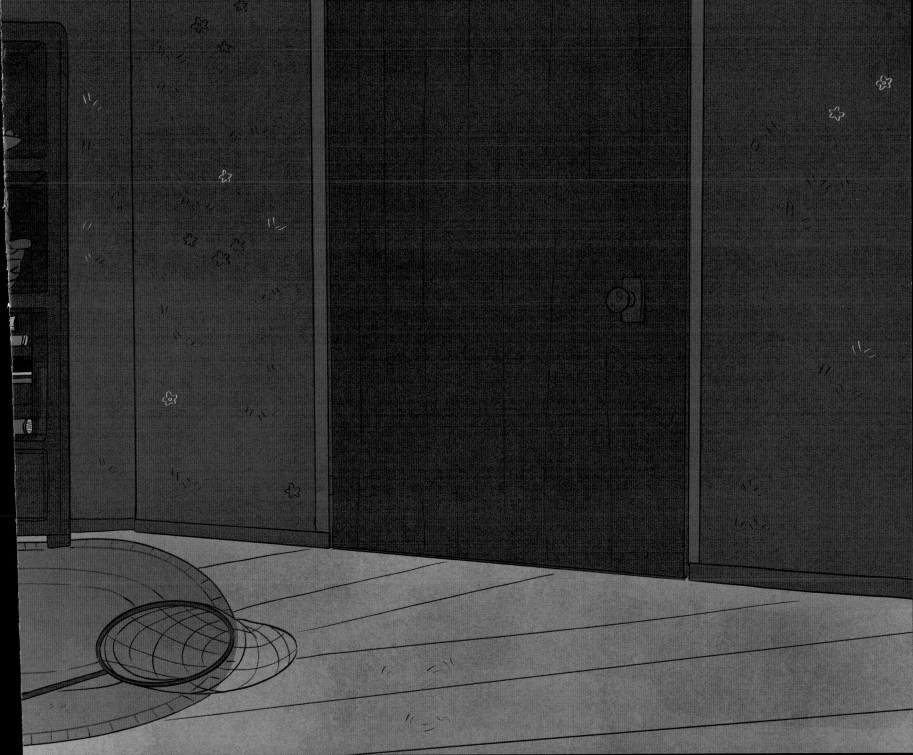

CReeeeeak

To Mike, for always believing in me.
– A.T.

Library of Congress Cataloging-in-Publication Data Available
ISBN 978-1-338-75565-7

10 9 8 7 6 5 4 3 2 1   22 23 24 25 26
Printed in China   38
First edition, August 2022
Alina Tysoe's illustrations were created digitally.
The display type was hand lettered.
The text type was set in Gotham Rounded.
The book was bound at RR Donnelley Asia.
Production was overseen by Catherine Weening
Manufacturing was supervised by Shannon Rice.
The book was art directed by Patti Ann Harris, designed by
Doan Buu, and edited by Kait Feldmann and Jess Harold.